1. This book may be kept three weeks.
   It is to be returned on / before the last date
   stamped below.
2. A fine of 20p will be charged for every week
   or part of week a book is overdue.

DOG STAR

*To Marty, the dog star had always looked
much the same as any other star.*

Dog Star

Written by
JENNY NIMMO

Illustrated by
TERRY MILNE

WALKER BOOKS
AND SUBSIDIARIES

LONDON • BOSTON • SYDNEY

This book was written for Wendy, with love

First published 1999 by Walker Books Ltd
87 Vauxhall Walk, London SE11 5HJ

2 4 6 8 10 9 7 5 3 1

Text © 1999 Jenny Nimmo
Illustrations © 1999 Terry Milne

This book has been typeset in Plantin Light.

Printed in England by Clays Ltd, St Ives plc

British Library Cataloguing in Publication Data
A catalogue record for this book is
available from the British Library.

ISBN 0-7445-5900-6 (hb)
ISBN 0-7445-7701-2 (pb)

CONTENTS

Marty followed her dad's finger,
and found the dog star.

To Marty, the dog star had always looked much the same as any other star. It had given no hint of the amazing part it would play in her life. And then, when she was eight and a half, something extraordinary happened.

It was a frosty January night and the stars were very bright. Marty was standing at the bottom of her garden trying to count them. She could hear her Uncle George sneezing in the house next door, but otherwise it was very quiet.

"Can you see Orion, the hunter?" said Marty's dad as he came crunching over the grass towards her.

Marty shook her head. She could see no hunters.

"There!" Her dad pointed into the glittery sky. "See the three stars on his belt!"

Marty gazed and gazed at the millions of stars. She couldn't make out Orion's shape at all. But she could see the stars on his belt, twinkling in a neat row round his waist.

"Now follow the line of his belt," said her dad, "down, down until you reach the hills. And there's Orion's dog. The dog star."

Marty followed her dad's finger, and found the dog star. It was so bright she wondered how she could have missed it.

"It flashes!" she said. "Pink, blue, purple, white. It's beautiful."

"Beautiful," agreed her dad. "The brightest star in the sky. It's the best time of the year to see it. D'you know it's taken eight and a half years for all those flashing colours to reach us. That's how far away it is."

Marty couldn't get her mind round that at all. But she liked the name, dog star. She'd always wanted a dog. "If I had a dog I would call it Star," she said. "It would be a pale gold colour, and it would have long silky hair and eyes as dark as midnight. And it would flash across the—"

"Hold on, Marty." Her dad sighed. "You know we can't have a dog. The cat would hate it. She'd run away."

"Tiggy's too old to run," said Marty grimly. "He's too old to do anything."

Her older sister Clare had crept up on them. She grabbed Marty's hand and drew her back to the house. "Marty's freezing," Clare told their dad. "You should have made her put her coat on."

Marty and Clare didn't have a mother, so

Clare, being three years older than Marty, thought she should behave like one. Clare could remember their mother, but Marty couldn't. "She departed this life the day you were born," Clare was fond of saying. "Still, no use crying over spilt milk."

Marty didn't think "spilt milk" was quite the way to describe a tragedy. But she supposed Clare knew best.

"You must start remembering things for yourself," Clare scolded. "You know Dad's hopeless. Look at him out there with only a shirt on."

"He needs a wife to look after him," said Marty.

"He does not." Clare didn't like the thought of another woman in the house. "He's got me," she said.

Marty thought that a daughter wasn't quite the same as a wife. But she kept her thoughts to herself. She didn't want to upset Clare, who could be a bit fiery at times. Besides, after cousin Rob, Clare was her best friend.

When Marty went to bed she found that the dog star had moved across the hills. Now it was beaming straight into her room. She opened her window and stared at the brilliant star. "Eight and a half years," she murmured, and imagined something setting out on its long journey through space; something that was born, perhaps, at the very same moment that she was born.

In the middle of the night Marty woke up. Her window was banging and a sudden gust of wind swept the curtains aside. A shaft of light cut through the room, from the window to the bed. And then everything was dark and still.

For a moment Marty was too scared to

move. Something had flown into her room. Very slowly Marty leaned over the bed and felt underneath. She touched a pencil, a book. Nothing else. And then she heard something. It was a very faint sound, no more than a whisper really. It was the sound of an animal, breathing. Under her bed.

Theresa Tree said, "Hello!" and got up from the table.
She was the tallest woman that Marty had ever seen.

CHAPTER TWO

Next morning Marty spooned some of Tiggy's cat food on to a saucer. She was about to carry it up to her room when Clare said, "What's that for?"

"My dog," said Marty, airily.

Clare rolled her eyes and looked at their dad, who was reading his paper. "You haven't brought a dirty stray in, have you?"

"Nope!" Marty ran out before Clare could get worked up.

She was just pushing the saucer under the bed when she heard Clare walk up behind her. "Where did it come from?" asked Clare.

15

Marty didn't know how to explain. She decided to tell the truth, as far as she knew it. "A star," she said.

Clare frowned. Then she knelt beside Marty and peered under the bed. "I can't see anything," she said.

"Of course you can't," said Marty. "It's too dark, and he's moved right to the back."

Clare stood up, brushing her knees. "He's very quiet."

"Silent," agreed Marty. "He's a silent dog, so he won't upset Tiggy."

"Oh, Marty," Clare gave one of her grown-up smiles. "There isn't a dog. You're just pretending."

"You don't have to believe me. I *know* I've got a dog. His name is Star, and he lives under my bed. Now, if you'll excuse me, I'm going to school." Marty slung her bag over her shoulder and ran downstairs.

Her cousin Rob was waiting for her at the gate. "What's up?" he asked as Marty came marching out.

"I've got a dog," growled Marty.

"I thought you wanted a dog." Rob fell into step beside her.

"I did," said Marty.

"So, why are you cross?"

"Clare doesn't believe me."

"Why?"

"Because she can't see it."

"Why?"

"Why, why, why," said Marty. "Can't you think of something different to say? Clare can't see it because it's under my bed, where it's very dark."

"Oh. Could I see it?" asked Rob. "I mean, will it come out so that I can meet it?"

"We'll see," said Marty.

They parted at the school gates. Rob

rushed off to join in a game of football at the far end of the playground while Marty wandered into her classroom.

All day she sat with her head in her hands, thinking. She hardly heard a word anyone said. She kept wondering if Star would still be there when she got home. She hadn't really seen him that morning. She had just sort of guessed that he was there.

When the school bell went, Marty sprang into life. She swept through the yard like a whirlwind. Auntie Jean had to catch hold of her bag to stop her tumbling into the road.

"Where d'you think you're going, Marty Marsh?" cried Auntie Jean. "You're supposed to wait for Rob and me."

"I've got to get home," panted Marty. "To feed my dog."

"Dog?" Auntie Jean looked very surprised. "Your dad said he'd never get a dog. All that barking will scare Tiggy out of his wits."

"My dog is a silent dog," Marty told her aunt. "His name is Star."

"And I'm going to meet him," said Rob, who'd just come running up.

"Can I come too?" asked Auntie Jean.

Marty shook her head. "Not yet. Not until he's used to being here. A crowd would scare him."

"I see. Well, I'm coming in anyway," said Auntie Jean. "Your dad's going to be late home today."

While Auntie Jean began to fix tea, Marty opened another tin of cat food and took Rob up to see Star. The saucer she had left by the bed was empty. "He's eaten it," Marty whispered.

"Why are you whispering?" whispered Rob, kneeling beside her.

"In case he's scared." Marty spooned some more cat food into the saucer and waited. "Star," she whispered.

Nothing happened. No black nose appeared. No whiskers. Not even a paw.

"Star doesn't seem hungry," said Rob. He peered under the bed. "I can't see him."

"Of course you can't. He's right at the back."

Rob began to put his arm under the bed and Marty cried, "Don't! He's not used to this place, yet. He might bite."

Rob quickly withdrew his hand. "Where did you get him?" he asked.

"He just came," said Marty.

"Through the door, just like that?"

"Through the window, actually," said Marty.

Rob stared at her. Marty stared back. She knew that Rob was going to say something she didn't want to hear, like *I don't believe you*, or *That's impossible*, so she very quickly said, "There is a dog under my bed. Listen!"

They both listened and, yes, there it was, very faint but unmistakable, the sound of an animal breathing.

"You see," said Marty softly. "You do believe he's there, don't you?"

Rob nodded. "Definitely."

They went downstairs, very quietly, so as not to frighten Star. While they had been in Marty's room something rather unusual had happened downstairs. There was a strange woman sitting at the kitchen table. Auntie Jean was looking very pleased, and so was Mr Marsh, but Clare had a face like thunder.

The strange woman smiled at Rob and Marty, and Mr Marsh said, "Marty, this is Miss Theresa Tree."

Theresa Tree said, "Hello!" and got up from the table. Up and up and up. It seemed that she would never stop. She was the tallest woman that Marty had ever seen. But she had a sweet face. "I've lost my dog," she said, "and I thought he might have come in here?"

Marty and Tiggy listened together.
And there it was. Star's soft, musical breathing.

CHAPTER THREE

"Why?" asked Marty, rather rudely.

Theresa didn't seem at all offended. She moved her chair to make room for Rob and Marty. "Someone said they'd seen him run through your gate," she said. "I was just looking in the bushes by the fence when your dad came home and found me." She glanced shyly at Mr Marsh. "And now here I am, having tea with you."

Mr Marsh gave her a big smile and pulled his chair closer to hers.

Rob and Marty sat down.

Marty could feel her heart thumping.

Please, please don't let Theresa's dog be Star, she said to herself. Taking a deep breath, she asked, "What does your dog look like, Miss Tree?"

"Please call me Theresa," said the visitor. "He's a large black labrador, very noisy and very friendly. A bit clumsy, though. He's called Rats."

Marty let out a big sigh of relief. "My dog's a lovely pale gold colour," she told Theresa. "His coat's long and silky and he's called Star."

"How lovely," said Theresa.

"What dog?" asked Mr Marsh, tearing his gaze away from Theresa.

"I told you this morning," said Marty patiently. "But you didn't listen. I've got a dog. His name is Star, and he won't upset Tiggy one bit, because he's a silent dog." Her dad's mouth opened, and Marty added hastily, "He doesn't bark, or chase cats!"

She hoped her dad was going to leave it at that but, of course, he had to ask, "Where did he come from?"

"I think he came from the star you showed me," Marty said quietly, "the dog star."

"Ah!" Dad looked at Auntie Jean, who smiled and looked at Clare, who was so angry about something she just shut her mouth tight, in a thin grim line.

"Shouldn't you be out looking for your dog?" Clare said to Theresa Tree. She spoke very sharply, not at all like the kind Clare that Marty was used to.

"We rang the police and the pets' rescue centre," said Theresa. "They're all keeping an eye out for him."

"Then you'd better go and wait by your phone, hadn't you?" said Clare coldly.

Theresa Tree looked at Mr Marsh. They

smiled at each other and Theresa said, "Your dad very kindly gave them this number."

Crack! Marty could hear Clare's teeth crunch as her mouth snapped shut. What was the matter with her?

There was a long silence while Auntie Jean poured tea and everybody else tucked into cheesy toast and beans.

Rob nudged Marty and whispered, "What's wrong with Clare?"

Clare heard her name and darted such a fierce look across the table, Marty was too scared to answer him. After tea, when Auntie Jean and Rob were leaving, Theresa picked up a tea-towel and said, "I'll dry up."

"No!" Clare snatched the tea-towel, her eyes blazing.

Rob rolled his eyes at Marty and said, "See you tomorrow."

Marty wished he would stay a bit longer. She didn't want to be left alone with Dad and Theresa and Clare. There was a cold, uncomfortable feeling in the house.

As soon as the front door closed, the telephone rang. Mr Marsh picked up the receiver. His face went glum. "It's for you," he told Theresa. "I'm afraid Rats has had an accident."

Theresa's eyes were already brimming as she listened to the voice on the other end of the line. "Thank you for letting me know," she said in a tiny voice. And then the tears came. A great flood of them.

Mr Marsh gently replaced the receiver and then he led Theresa into the sitting-room. They both collapsed on the sofa and Theresa sobbed and sobbed on to his shoulder.

Clare and Marty looked in on them.

"Sounds as though Rats has had it," said the new, cold Clare.

Marty was shocked. "Poor Rats," she whispered. "And poor Theresa."

"Poor Theresa," said Clare heartlessly, and she marched off to watch the television in her bedroom.

Marty didn't have her own TV. But she did have a dog. She ran upstairs and found Tiggy sitting just outside her door. He looked very odd. Not scared. Not angry, but sort of puzzled.

"Have you met Star?" asked Marty.

Tiggy looked at her, head on one side, ears forward. He purred. It was hard to tell if this was an answer.

"Come in," Marty invited. "I'll introduce you." She noticed that Star's saucer was empty.

Tiggy followed Marty into her room. He

was a very old cat with masses of long brown and white fur. They'd had to have an extra-large cat-flap made for him, because he was so wide. Long ago he'd been a sweet little kitten, a present from Mr Marsh to his future wife. This made him very precious.

"Now, sit here!" Marty pulled Tiggy on to her lap. "And listen!"

They listened together. And there it was. Star's soft, musical breathing. Tiggy looked up at Marty and purred.

"You like him," said Marty. "I knew you would. Now three of us know about him. You and me and Rob."

Tiggy rubbed his head on Marty's arm and walked off.

Marty heard Theresa say goodbye, then the front door closed and the house went very quiet. Marty looked into Clare's room. Her sister was hunched in front of the TV.

"Are you angry about something?" Marty asked.

Clare didn't reply.

"'Night, then," said Marty.

"'Night," mumbled Clare.

Marty went to find her dad. He was sitting in the kitchen and he looked all dreamy. When Marty spoke he didn't seem to hear her. Or see her. Even when she plonked a kiss on his cheek, he just sort of smiled over her shoulder.

"'Night, Marty," he murmured as she left the room.

The house felt empty even though three people were living in it. Three people and a cat.

And a dog!

Marty bounded upstairs feeling better. "At least you're here!" she whispered to the shadows beneath her bed.

It was a cold, cloudy night. Marty couldn't see any stars at all. When she switched off her light, the room was plunged into such utter darkness it made her shiver. And then something happened. Tiny threads of light trickled across the floor: a gleaming, golden light. Marty lay perfectly still and watched the gleam creep over her shoes, her books, her folded clothes. For a moment she thought it was moonlight, but there was no moon. The glow was coming from under her bed.

Marty had always imagined the light from a star to be very cold, like tiny icicles. But Star's light was warm and friendly, and his quiet breathing was as comforting as a hug.

Worst of all was the flag on the tower of scones.
"Clare!" roared Mr Marsh. "Did you do this?"

CHAPTER FOUR

On Saturday, Mr Marsh said, "We're having a visitor to tea, so I want the house to be really clean."

"I can guess who the visitor is," said Clare. "Terribly Tall Theresa Tree."

"As a matter of fact, it is." Mr Marsh grinned like the cat that got the cream. "But please don't make fun of her height."

"She has a pretty face," said Marty helpfully.

"How can you tell?" muttered Clare. "It's so high up."

Mr Marsh lost his grin. "I want you to make Theresa feel welcome," he said. "She's very down after poor Rats was run over."

Clare huffed and swung away.

Marty had always enjoyed the Saturday clean-up. Her dad whistled as he hoovered, Clare sang as she swept and Marty would hum along with both of them while she dusted and polished and wiped. In no time at all the house would be spick and span; windows sparkling, wet clothes flapping on the line and piles of ironing, crisp and fresh in the kitchen. And Dad would say, "What a family! Aren't we great?"

Today things were different. Dad whistled but Clare didn't sing, and that made Marty feel she couldn't. So, after a while, Dad's whistling just faded away. Now and again he'd say "Da-di-da!" just to keep things going, but it sounded rather half-hearted.

Mr Marsh was very good at baking, which was just as well as he was a baker. For tea he made a large carrot cake, a jam sponge and a chocolate roll. Marty helped him to make the scones: twenty-four of them, and the sandwiches: thirty, cut in neat triangles.

"A bit over the top, I'd say," Clare remarked. "We'll never eat all those. They'll just go mouldy."

Mr Marsh looked hurt. "Theresa loves cake," he said.

"Theresa should cut down on cake," said Clare spitefully. "She's too big already."

Marty couldn't bear the way they looked at each other. Dad and Clare. Angry and miserable.

"I'm sure Star would eat some," she said, hoping to improve the situation.

It didn't work. Now Dad and Clare were looking at her instead of each other. But at least Dad said, kindly, "That's good. I'd hate to waste prime ham. And perhaps Rob would come over."

"I'll go and ask."

As soon as Marty had left the room she heard Clare say, "You shouldn't encourage her. You know that dog doesn't exist."

"Where's the harm," said Mr Marsh, "if it makes Marty happy."

Marty stopped dead in her tracks. They didn't believe her. Neither of them. Not one bit. She rushed up to her room.

"Star!" she called. "Star, you are there, aren't you?"

There was a soft thump from under the bed. A tail thumping the floor? There it was again. *Thump! Thump! Thump!*

Marty lay beside her bed. If only she could see him. "I know you're there," she said, "of course I do. But couldn't you come out, just a bit, so I can see you!"

Star was either afraid or too shy. Perhaps,

he just didn't like daylight.

"Please," Marty begged, and she stretched her hand as far as she could, under the bed.

She could hear Star panting very fast, as though he'd been running, or doing some hard thinking. Then, suddenly, a little cloud of sparks blew out of the shadows and settled on her hand. They made a soft crackling sound, like the sparks that flew from her hair when she brushed it extra hard.

Marty regarded her hand. The sparks had vanished but they left a lovely tingle on her skin. "I understand," said Marty. "You're not quite ready, are you? I'll bring you some cake after tea, or perhaps you'd prefer a ham sandwich."

She ran next door to fetch Rob and by the time they got back, Theresa Tree had arrived. She looked really pretty, with her black hair tied back and long green earrings gleaming beside her cheeks.

Mr Marsh was entertaining his guest in the sitting-room. He had that strange, dreamy look on his face again. This time Theresa didn't stand up like a tower, she just stayed where she was and said, "Well, here I am again."

"You're very welcome," said Marty, remembering what her dad had told her.

"Tea's up!" called Clare, and everyone moved into the kitchen.

Clare had covered the table with a lacy cloth and it looked very smart. A red paper napkin lay beside each place, and the cakes sat on silver doilies. Every plate of food had a little flag on it, explaining what it was.

Marty peered at the flags, trying to make out what they said. She jumped back in horror, stepping on Rob's foot.

"Ouch!" cried Rob.

At the very same moment Mr Marsh gave a gasp of anger.

The flag on the chocolate cake said, "Watch out if you don't want spots!" The flag on the sponge cake said, "Cream is bad for the figure." The flag on the sandwiches said, "These sandwiches have pig in them."

But worst of all was the flag on the tower of scones: "Tall people shouldn't eat jam!"

"Clare!" roared Mr Marsh. "Did you do this?"

"Yes, I did," said Clare defiantly. "And as I don't want to get spots or grow fat or eat pig, I shall just eat a jam scone, because I'm not tall."

Mr Marsh went a dangerous shade of pink. Marty had never seen him look so angry. She grabbed Rob's hand and pulled him away from the table, afraid that her dad was going to explode.

Marty went to help her sister in the kitchen.
"What's the matter?" she asked Clare.

CHAPTER FIVE

Mr Marsh didn't explode. Before he could do anything, Theresa said, "What a good idea, putting labels on things. I shall eat everything except jam. After all, I don't want to grow any taller, do I?" She laughed.

Marty laughed with her, and so did Rob. Mr Marsh joined in, but Clare didn't even smile. She seemed to have lost track of the funny side of life.

She was right about one thing, though. Mr Marsh had gone over the top with his baking. There was a whole sponge cake, six ham sandwiches and masses of scones left over after tea.

"I'll take some sandwiches up to Star," said Marty. "Come on, Rob!"

Mr Marsh didn't hear her. He was gazing at Theresa, who was smiling fondly back at him. Clare was throwing things into the fridge.

They found Tiggy sitting beside Marty's open door. "He's always there, now," said Marty. "I think he likes Star."

"He's the only one who's seen him," Rob remarked. "I mean, he's the only thing small enough to get under your bed," he glanced at fat Tiggy. "Well, perhaps not."

"I've seen Star," Marty said, and then she realized that she hadn't, not really. But she knew what he looked like. There was absolutely no doubt in her mind at all. "Just once," she added.

She slipped the plate of sandwiches under

the bed, just at the edge where she and Rob could see it. Then they both sat on the floor and waited.

Rob looked rather forlorn and to cheer him up Marty said, "I'm sure he'll come out soon. Everything's still so strange to him, he's a bit scared." And she told Rob about the tiny sparks that had covered her hand the night before.

"You're so lucky," Rob sighed. "There'll be no pets for me – ever. Dad's allergic to them. I can't even have a budgie or gerbil."

"You can come and play with Star," Marty offered. "Anytime you like."

"When he comes out," said Rob, looking happier.

"When he comes out," said Marty, trying to banish a niggling doubt. Suppose Star never came out. He certainly wasn't ready to show himself yet. After ten minutes of silent watching they decided to leave him to have his tea in peace.

Clare was banging about in the kitchen when they went downstairs. "Dad's taken Terribly Tall Theresa home," she said, tossing a pile of knives into a drawer. They made a deafening clatter.

"I think I'll go home," said Rob. "There's something I want to see on telly."

When he'd gone Marty went to help her sister in the kitchen. "What's the matter?" she asked Clare. "You've looked cross ever since yesterday."

"Why d'you think?" snapped Clare.

"You don't like Theresa, do you?"

"I think Dad's fallen in love with her."

"What?" Marty was stunned. "Just like that? In two days?"

"It happens," said Clare. "He doesn't realize that she's quite the wrong sort of person for him."

"Because she's so tall?" asked Marty.

"There are lots of reasons," said Clare. "She's a stranger, she's too young, too tall and she doesn't fit in here."

"She could fit in," said Marty. "She's very friendly."

Clare wheeled round from the sink. "Look, we don't need a mother! Dad doesn't need a wife, or a girlfriend! Get it?"

"Yes," said Marty meekly. "But it would be good if—"

"I don't want you making friends with her," said Clare.

"But I—"

"No! No! No!" Clare looked so fierce Marty fled upstairs.

She found that Star had eaten every sandwich on his plate. Marty took the empty plate down to the kitchen. "Look!" she said, happily waving the empty plate. "I think ham must be Star's favourite food. He's eaten every bit."

She had hoped this news would drive away the little clouds of bitterness that hung about her angry sister. She'd hoped that Clare would smile again and everything would be all right.

Clare did smile, but it was a heartless, mocking smile. "Oh, Marty," she said, "Tiggy's been eating the food under your bed. Didn't you realize? That's why he sits by your door all day. There is no dog. Star doesn't exist."

For a moment Marty was too shocked to speak. Hot tears stung her eyelids and she whispered, "He does exist. I'll prove it."

As she ran upstairs she saw Tiggy giving himself a good wash on the top step. Marty swung him into her arms and, carrying him to the front door, she thrust him out into the cold garden.

Oww! Oww! Oww! mewed Tiggy.

Deaf to his pleading, Marty slammed the door, closed the cat-flap and bolted it firmly.

"Now we'll see." Marty dashed into the kitchen, grabbed a saucer and spooned some cat food into it. "You'll eat your words," she said to her startled sister and ran upstairs.

"*Please* eat this," she said, and laying her head on the floor she searched the shadows under her bed.

A faint breath stole towards her, then a tiny, distant thump.

"I've got to make them believe," said Marty softly, "so please!" She tiptoed away, closing the door behind her, and went to watch TV in the sitting-room. But the outraged Tiggy's wails drifted round the house, and even when Marty turned up the volume on the television, she couldn't drown them out.

All at once, the sitting-room door burst open and Mr Marsh strode up to Marty. Tiggy was clinging to his shoulder.

"Did you lock Tiggy out?" he demanded.

"Yes," said Marty weakly.

"Marty, how could you? It's freezing out there. Tiggy's a very old cat."

"Clare said he was eating Star's food," murmured Marty.

Mr Marsh frowned. He looked puzzled and sad. "Poor Tiggy. He can't help it. He's too old to hunt, now. What d'you expect if you leave food on the floor. He can't resist it."

"But Tiggy didn't eat the food," Marty explained, in a small voice. "Star ate it. I just locked Tiggy out to prove it."

Mr Marsh looked even more puzzled, then he shook his head. "I'm sorry, Marty." He gave her a faraway look and carried Tiggy away.

What did he mean, "Sorry"? Was he apologizing or telling her she was wrong? Marty went to see if Star had eaten the cat food. He hadn't. A little shiver crept down her spine.

She lay on her bed and closed her eyes. "I don't suppose you were hungry, were you?" she murmured. "You're full of sandwiches."

When she opened her eyes the room was very warm. There was a soft glow on her carpet and, beneath the bed, just where Marty's head was resting, there came a gentle throb of life.

"I *knew* you were there," Marty whispered.

Clare said, "Marty, I want to talk to you!"
They sat side by side on the bed.

CHAPTER SIX

Theresa Tree came round twice the following week. Every time she came something nasty happened.

On the first occasion, Theresa's scarf disappeared. "Please, don't worry," said Theresa. "It was only an old one."

Marty knew this wasn't true. It was a beautiful scarf, patterned with tiny flowers and butterflies. That evening Mr Marsh found the scarf in a bucket of bleach with the dishcloths. The colours on the scarf had completely faded.

"Oh, dear," said Clare. "I must have picked it up with the dishcloths. I wonder how I managed to do that?"

"I wonder!" Mr Marsh gave her a sad look. "I'll buy Theresa a new scarf," he said, "with your pocket money."

Clare scowled and huffed and stomped off.

The next time Theresa came to visit, Clare accidentally knocked a jug of milk over. The milk dripped on to Theresa's black velvet trousers.

"Oh, sorry!" said Clare. "I wonder how I managed to do that."

"I wonder," said Mr Marsh grimly.

"I'd lend you my jeans to go home in," Clare told Theresa, "only you're much too tall. I expect it's difficult for you to find clothes that fit."

"I make them myself," said Theresa, dabbing her trousers with a cloth, "so it's no problem."

"How brilliant," Marty exclaimed. "I wish I could make clothes."

"I'll teach you," said Theresa.

"Wow!" cried Marty. She tried not to look at Clare, who was scowling and banging stuff about.

Theresa said, "When I come to see you on Saturday, I'll bring some scissors and a paper pattern. What's your favourite colour?"

"Red," said Marty.

"We'll make a red skirt, then," said Theresa.

"Yes!" cried Marty. "And maybe, just maybe, my dog Star will come right out from under the bed and you can meet him."

"Great!" said Theresa.

Dad's smile had come back. The smile that stretched right across his face, and Marty thought: everything's going to be all right. But when Theresa had gone, Clare followed Marty up to her room.

Marty noticed that Star's saucer of food was empty. The door had been closed so Tiggy couldn't have got it. She was about to tell Clare this, but Clare said, "Marty, I want to talk to you!"

They sat side by side on the bed.

"It's about Theresa," Clare began.

"She wasn't cross about the milk, was she?" Marty said quickly. Some people would have been.

"She's never going to be cross," said Clare. "Not until she's got Dad to marry her and moved in. Then he'll be under her thumb and so will we. She'll make our lives a misery, stepmothers always do."

"I don't think—"

"Believe me," Clare said sternly. "Remember Snow White!"

"Theresa's not like that!" Marty protested.

Clare stood up. "If you make friends with her, I'll never speak to you again. In fact, I'll leave this house."

"What?" Marty was horrified. "Where will you go?" she asked in a stricken voice. "You're not even a teenager."

"I'll go to Scotland," Clare informed her, "where Dad's cousin Morag lives."

Marty remembered Morag's Christmas card. Dad said Scotland was hundreds of miles away.

"Don't look so scared." Clare gave Marty a hug. "I'll only go if Terribly Tall Theresa moves in. But we're not going to let that happen, are we?"

"No," whispered Marty.

"Because we're going to drive her away, aren't we, Marty?"

Marty thought of the red skirt she and Theresa were going to make. She couldn't speak, so she just nodded miserably.

"I knew I could rely on you." Clare bounced out of the room, her face quite free of the scowl she'd been wearing lately.

"What shall I do?" Marty murmured.

A faint but definite sigh reached Marty. It could have been the tree outside her window, or the bed springs, or even a draught slipping under the door. She knew it was none of these things. It was Star's way of warning her.

"I don't want Clare to leave home," she said. "I have to do what she wants … otherwise … otherwise … what would I do without her?"

There was no sound from under the bed. No answer.

"You're not much help, are you?" Marty

grumbled. "And anyway, how do I know you exist?"

She walked out, quite forgetting the empty saucer, and the cat food that Tiggy couldn't possibly have eaten.

As the big cat wandered back to his nook a
soft glow began to slide down the stairs.

CHAPTER SEVEN

Marty forgot to wait for Rob in the morning.

"How's Star?" he cried, running up behind her.

"He's quiet," said Marty.

"Is he still eating?"

"Yes."

"Does he go to the toilet?"

Marty hadn't thought about this. "Yes," she decided. "He gets through the cat-flap when no one's looking, and goes in the garden."

"Ah yes, of course," said Rob. "Can I come and see him on Saturday?"

"No," said Marty.

"Why?" Rob looked very upset.

"Because Theresa Tree is coming to tea."

"So?"

"Clare doesn't want me to talk to her."

"Why?"

"You're doing it again," grumbled Marty. "Why? Why? Why?"

"Sorry." Rob kicked the pavement.

"It's going to be a horrible day," Marty explained. "But I suppose you can come."

"I don't want to now," said Rob.

When Theresa came in she carried a shiny green bag with gold and black letters on the front – *Fox's Fine Fabrics*.

Marty's heart sank.

Theresa thrust her hand in the bag and brought out a length of red velvet. "The best in the shop," she declared. "It'll make a lovely skirt. D'you like it, Marty?"

Such a rich ruby red it was, and so soft and beautiful. Marty thought of the birthday parties that were coming up. She'd always wanted a red skirt.

"Well, Marty?" said Mr Marsh anxiously. "Say something."

Marty could feel Clare's sharp grey eyes on her, watching and waiting. She imagined Clare flinging on her coat and marching out. Never to return.

"I don't want it," Marty said.

Theresa stared at her. Mr Marsh's mouth hung open. "What?" he croaked.

"It's very nice," Marty said quietly, "but I don't need another skirt. I've got tons."

"I see." Sadly, Theresa dropped the velvet back into the bag. "Never mind." She forced a smile on to her face; an awkward, downcast smile.

Marty couldn't look at her or anyone else.

Clare was grinning and Mr Marsh was staring at his feet.

"I'm tired," said Marty. "I'm going to lie down."

"You can watch the TV in my room, if you like," Clare said sweetly.

Marty muttered, "No thanks!"

Theresa didn't stay very long. Marty stood at her bedroom window and watched her leave. For a tall person she walked very gracefully. She looked like a willow, or a fir tree with feathery branches. "She barely had time for a cup of tea," Marty remarked.

But if Star was listening he had nothing to say.

Mr Marsh walked down the garden path and stood at the gate. He gazed in the direction that Theresa had taken. And then he looked into the sky, as though he were searching for stars. But even the stars were unfriendly tonight. Not one had bothered to fight its way through the clouds.

There was a tap on Marty's door and Clare walked in, carrying a plate of sandwiches. "I thought you might like something to eat," she said.

"I'm not hungry," Marty told her.

"Well, give them to your dog, then."

"You don't believe in my dog," said Marty.

"I didn't say that, exactly."

Marty decided to change the subject. "Theresa didn't stay long."

"No. You were just great." Clare gave her a hug. "She really got the message this time."

"Did she?"

Clare put the sandwiches on the floor by Marty's bed. "I'm going to leave these here in case you change your mind!" She skipped away looking very happy.

Marty didn't feel happy. She didn't feel great either. She had a funny ache in her stomach, the sort of ache that gives you nightmares.

"I bet I won't sleep a wink tonight," she said to herself. As a matter of fact, Marty was so tired she slept very soundly.

In the middle of the night Tiggy crept out of his hiding place in the bathroom. He had a nice warm nook behind the pipes that no one knew about. Tiggy had seen Clare carry the sandwiches into Marty's room; they smelt of tuna and chicken, both Tiggy's favourites.

Marty's door was open. Tiggy looked in. The plate by the bed was empty. Tiggy turned away, disappointed.

As the big cat wandered back to his nook, something brushed past him. A soft glow, like a slice of starlight, began to glide down the stairs.

"Oh, it's you," said Tiggy. "I suppose you ate the sandwiches." The glimmering dog-shape stopped for a moment and looked back, regretfully. Then it moved on, across the hall to the cat-flap.

"Don't go," mewed Tiggy softly. "I'll miss you!" But the dog had vanished into the night.

"Which way?" Rob spluttered. "This way," Marty decided, choosing the direction that Theresa had taken.

CHAPTER EIGHT

The minute she woke up, Marty knew that something was wrong. She felt as though she were lying on emptiness. It wasn't the emptiness that would have made her feel she was flying, it was more like a dreadful nothingness; a black hole which she might drop through, right to the bottom of the house, where she'd land with a bump.

Swinging her legs out of bed, Marty stared at the floor. It was still there. No hole. She knew what the nothingness was. It was the empty place under her bed. Star had gone. She saw the plate that had been piled high with sandwiches. All gone. He'd had one last meal and left. It was obvious.

Marty threw on her clothes. Her socks didn't match, her jumper was inside out and her shoelaces weren't properly tied. But she was too troubled to care.

"Where? Where? Where?" she moaned, running downstairs.

It was no use telling Dad and Clare. They didn't believe in Star. Anyway, they were sound asleep. Only two people believed in her dog. Theresa and Rob. Theresa would probably never speak to her again.

Marty put on her coat and ran next door. Luckily, Rob was an early riser. He always made his own breakfast on Sundays: a giant bowl of strawberry flakes. He opened the door dribbling coloured milk down his chin. "Wash-a-matter?" he asked, seeing Marty's panicky face.

"Star's gone!" said Marty.

"Where?"

"How do I know!" she cried.

"Joo-wah-me-t'elp-you-look?"

"Yes, please," said Marty gratefully.

Rob swallowed his mouthful and started coughing. He was still coughing when they ran through the gate.

"Which way?" Rob spluttered.

"This way," Marty decided, choosing the direction that Theresa had taken. "Into the town." A bitter wind blew tiny hailstones in their faces and every puddle had a thin glaze of ice.

"Why d'you think he ran away?" asked Rob with another cough.

"I don't know," cried Marty, wildly. "Perhaps it was because I was mean to Theresa. But Clare made me."

Rob was about to ask why, but he didn't

want to add to Marty's troubles. He knew she hated him saying "why", so he said, "D'you always do what Clare tells you to?"

"Yes," said Marty, putting her foot through a sheet of ice.

"Wh…" Rob had to stop himself asking why.

Marty glanced at him. "You look very peculiar," she said. "What's the matter with your mouth?"

Rob tried to find a way out of his difficulty. "Well, I just think it's silly, always doing what your sister says, even if you know it's wrong."

Marty ignored this. She ran even faster, peering in gardens, calling Star's name and asking everyone she met, "Have you seen my dog, Star? He's medium-sized with a pale gold coat, long and floaty, and a feathery tail like a comet. Oh, and he

72

doesn't bark."

The people she asked weren't very helpful. They said things like, "Should have kept it on a lead." "Has it got a name on its collar?" "No collar?" "Shame!" "Stray dogs cause accidents."

In the end they asked a policeman, who seemed more worried about them than a runaway dog. He took them home in his panda car.

Mr Marsh, Auntie Jean and Clare were in a dreadful state. They were all in the Marshes' kitchen. One minute they were hugging Rob and Marty, and the next they were angry with them. Clare had been crying.

"Where have you been?" "Why did you go?" "What were you thinking of?" "Why didn't you tell us?" These were only some of the questions fired at the runaway children.

"Star ran away, not us," Marty explained. "We were searching for him."

"Star?" Mr Marsh looked puzzled.

"My dog," cried Marty. "My lovely, sparkling, beautiful golden dog."

"Oh, your dog," said Mr Marsh, Auntie Jean and Clare.

Marty began to cry.

Auntie Jean gave her a squeeze and said, "I expect he'll come back on his own." Then she took Rob home.

"You forgot your gloves and your coat's not done up," Clare said in her motherly voice. "And look at your shoes, they're wet! You'd better go and change them."

Marty trudged upstairs.

Tiggy was sitting on the landing, looking all forlorn. "You miss him too, don't you?" Marty said.

Miaow! Tiggy sadly agreed.

It was freezing in Marty's room. And so very, very empty. "I'll never feel warm again," she said to herself.

She spent the rest of the day rubbing her hands by the fire and shivering. At bedtime she had to ask Clare for an extra blanket.

"You've caught a chill," said Clare, "rushing outside in the cold, with your coat flying open and no scarf."

But Marty knew it was more than a chill. It was the cold of sadness, of missing something so much that it froze her inside and out.

When she saw Rob next morning, she felt it was like looking in a mirror. "You look just like I feel," she said. "I miss Star so much I don't think I'll ever be happy again."

"Perhaps he'll come back like Mum said," Rob suggested. "All by himself. He might even come back tonight."

But Star didn't come back.

Every day Rob and Marty talked about the things they would do when Star came back. They would take him for walks in the park. They would buy a ball and play football with him. They would teach him road safety and give him lessons in hygiene (toilet training).

And then, one day, Marty couldn't bear it any longer. "He's not going to come back," she said. "Never, never, never. Because he thinks I don't believe in him."

"But you do," said Rob, "and so do I. How can we let him know?"

"We can't," said Marty.

At the end of the week a parcel arrived for Marty. When she opened it she found a red velvet skirt, just her size. A note was pinned to the pocket.

It said:

Dear Marty,

I know you didn't want another skirt, but it seemed a shame to waste such nice material. I guessed your size so I hope it fits. And I hope you like it.

Love from Theresa Tree

Marty tried it on in her bedroom. It was a perfect fit.

"You're not going to wear it, are you?" Clare looked in, disapprovingly.

"Yes," said Marty.

"But it came from Theresa Tree."

"It doesn't matter, does it?" Marty pleaded. "I mean, she isn't *in* the skirt, I am."

"Huh!" huffed Clare. "Just as long as she doesn't come back." She was about to go when she remembered something. "It's Dad's birthday next week. What shall we get him?"

Marty thought of the socks and shirts and

painted mugs they'd given Dad before: she remembered the plaster of Paris cats, the star book and the wooden paper-knife. None of these things would do this time.

"Well, what d'you think he'd like?" Clare asked.

"Theresa Tree," said Marty.

"Huh!" huffed Clare, and off she marched.

Marty went to find out what her father really wanted.

"I don't know, Marty," Mr Marsh said wearily. "I'm too old for birthdays. Socks will do very nicely."

"Would socks make you happy?"

Marty looked into her Dad's warm brown eyes and he looked into hers. She knew very well what would make him happy.

"Why didn't Theresa come back?" she asked.

Mr Marsh gazed at Marty's red skirt. He'd only just noticed it. "Well, we could see that you girls were upset about her and me being friends," he said. "And you mean the world to me, Marty – you and Clare. So we called it a day."

"But she sent me the skirt."

"So I see. It was very kind of her."

"Shall I write a thank you letter?" asked Marty.

"That would be nice." Mr Marsh brightened up a bit.

Marty went to her room and began the letter immediately.

Dear Theresa,
Thank you for the skirt. I love it.
I've lost my dog, Star. The one I told you about. He has got a pale gold coat and a tail like a comet. His eyes are as dark as midnight and he doesn't bark. I hope you are well.
Love, from Marty Marsh

Marty showed this part of the letter to her dad, to check for spelling mistakes. When he'd read it, she took her letter away and added something: It's Dad's birthday on Friday. Then she put it in an envelope with Theresa's name and address on it, and ran to the postbox at the end of the road.

When she got back, Clare said, "You look as if you're hiding something. What have you done, Marty?"

"Nothing," said Marty. "Nothing at all."

*Marty picked up Star in her arms and whirled
round the garden with her eyes closed tight.*

CHAPTER NINE

Theresa Tree passed the dogs' home every day on her way to work. She would hear the lost dogs calling from behind the high brick wall, and have to hurry by. She would have rescued them all if she hadn't had such a tiny garden.

Today, Theresa didn't hurry past the dogs' home. She wondered if she might find Marty's dog inside. She stopped and listened. Something was wrong. Not wrong, exactly. Different. There were no sounds at all coming from behind the high brick wall. The dogs' home was silent.

Had all the stray dogs run away? A strange

feeling came over Theresa. It was almost as if something she couldn't see was beckoning her. She turned into the entrance hall and rang the bell on the counter.

Her friend, Sharon, appeared at the end of a passage. She wore a navy blue overall and a badge with her name, pinned to her top pocket: Sharon Catt.

"Has something happened, Sharon?" asked Theresa.

"Not exactly," said Sharon mysteriously. "The vet's just checked all the dogs and they're fine, but…"

"Silent," said Theresa.

"Silent," agreed Sharon. "I was so sad to hear about Rats. Have you come to choose another dog?"

"I don't think so." Theresa rubbed her forehead. "I feel a bit peculiar, actually. Something made me come in here … oh, now I remember. A friend of mine has lost her dog, and I thought I might find him here."

"Come and see them." Sharon took Theresa to the row of pens where sad lost dogs were usually howling their hearts out.

Theresa walked down the row of pens. Today, all the dogs stood quietly wagging their tails. Their eyes were bright and they almost seemed to be smiling.

"They look very happy," said Theresa.

"And see how glossy their coats are," said Sharon. "They'll find new homes in no time if this carries on."

"It's almost like magic," said Theresa. "When did it start?"

"When the white dog came."

"The white dog?"

"Not white exactly, more a pale gold," Sharon explained. "I found him on the step the other night. When I opened the door he just walked in. It was almost as if he knew where to come."

"How strange," Theresa murmured.

"He's a bit of a star, he is," Sharon told her. "You'll find him at the end of the row."

Theresa's heart missed a beat. "What's happening to me?" she wondered. As she walked towards the last pen, she had the odd feeling of being beckoned again. Perhaps the spell that has worked its magic on the dogs has captured me as well, she thought.

She reached the very last pen. It appeared to be empty. And then she saw the dog. He was sitting in the shadowy kennel at the back. His pale coat seemed to glow; a star in the evening sky.

"Star!" said Theresa. "Is it you?"

The dog came towards her, his silky tail swinging gently. She could see that his coat had threads of gold in it. His eyes were as deep and dark as midnight.

Theresa knelt beside the pen and clutched the wire. The dog pressed his face against her fingers and she could feel his velvety coat. It was warm and curiously comforting.

"It's him," breathed Theresa.

"Are you sure?" asked Sharon.

"Oh, yes. I'm quite, quite sure," said Theresa.

Mr Marsh wasn't baking. It worried Marty. He always made his own birthday cake a week ahead, so that Clare and Marty could decorate it. But this year he just couldn't seem to get down to it.

Marty went next door to tell Auntie Jean. "I'll make the cake," she said.

"He doesn't have the heart for it," Marty told her aunt. "He says grown-ups shouldn't celebrate birthdays. But I like his birthdays as much as my own."

"We'll make everything here," said her aunt. "Then we'll carry it round and surprise him."

They heard Uncle George give a terrific sneeze from somewhere, and Auntie Jean said, "Poor George, his allergies seem to be getting worse. It's a good job we haven't got anything with fur in the house."

"We have," said Rob as he came through the door. Tiggy was purring in his arms. "I found him on my bed."

Auntie Jean screamed as if Tiggy were a time-bomb. "Why did he come in here?" she squeaked. "He doesn't like other people's houses."

"He misses Star," said Marty, taking Tiggy from Rob.

"Who?" asked Auntie Jean.

"STAR!" shouted Rob and Marty.

"Oh!" said Auntie Jean. "Well, please take Tiggy home and try to keep him there."

"I'll try," muttered Marty.

Mr Marsh's birthday loomed. Marty began to dread it. He wouldn't like the pen she'd bought. He wouldn't like the cakes they'd made. It was all going to be a dreadful disappointment.

It wasn't quite as bad as she'd imagined. Mr Marsh did like the pen.

"It's just what I wanted," he said, giving Marty a kiss, "a lovely silver pen. I can clip it on to my baker's apron."

He opened his presents at breakfast: a new apron from Clare, gloves from Rob and a bottle of champagne from Auntie Jean and Uncle George.

"I'm spoilt," said Mr Marsh.

Marty had hoped there would be

something from Theresa Tree, but there wasn't. Not even a card.

"You're going to have a party, you know," she said, trying to cheer him up. "But you'll have to wait until after school."

"Ah." Mr Marsh gave a wan smile.

Marty wished he could smile properly.

After school, Marty and Clare went straight to Auntie Jean's house. The birthday cake sat on the kitchen table, waiting to be decorated. The girls took turns in piping scarlet patterns round the edge, arranging silver balls and chocolate buttons, and fitting bright green candles into scarlet holders.

"We'll light the candles when we get there," said Auntie Jean, which was just as well because they had to carry the food through an icy wind. The clouds had blown away and the sky was crammed with very bright stars.

They walked single file, out through one gate and in through another. Marty first with the birthday cake, Uncle George last with a jelly. The jelly nearly wobbled off the plate every time he sneezed.

"What's your dad allergic to this time?" Marty asked Rob, walking behind with a trifle.

"Jelly," said Rob.

Mr Marsh opened the door with a great big smile that didn't have one ounce of happiness in it. Marty gave him ten out of ten for trying.

All through the birthday tea, Marty kept thinking: Everyone's trying so hard to be merry but they just can't seem to manage it. And then, before she could stop herself, the forbidden subject popped out. "The last time we had sandwiches, Theresa Tree was here, but she went home without her tea. And my dog Star ate all the sandwiches, and then he ran away." Two big tears rolled down her cheeks and she quickly brushed them away.

"Let's light the candles!" Auntie Jean jumped up and set to work with a match. Soon the cake was sparkling splendidly.

"Make a wish!" said Clare and Marty.

Mr Marsh closed his eyes while Uncle George tried to hold back his sneeze. An impossible task. "A-T-I-S-H-O-O!"

The tiny flames trembled and went out.

Everyone shouted angrily at Uncle George, but Mr Marsh said, "It doesn't matter, I'd already made my wish."

And then someone rang the doorbell.

A strange silence descended. They all looked startled. Who could it be?

"You answer it, Marty," said Mr Marsh.

Marty went into the hall. As she moved towards the door she began to tingle all over. Who was on the other side. Could it be…?

Marty opened the door. There on the shadowy path stood a tall figure. Theresa Tree. "Hello!" she said. "I think I've found your dog."

Marty couldn't speak. She could only gasp. For there, sitting at Theresa's feet, was a dog. A shining, pale gold dog with a long, feathery coat and eyes as dark as midnight.

"Star!" cried Marty. Before she could say another word the dog ran up to her and she was kneeling on the frosty grass, hugging, hugging and hugging him.

Then she picked up Star in her arms and whirled round the garden with her eyes closed tight. He was warm and silky and very, very real.

When she opened her eyes Mr Marsh and

Clare were standing in the open doorway.

"It's Star!" cried Marty. "Theresa found him." She carried him into the light that spilled from the open door, and set him down before them.

"He's very beautiful," Clare murmured. But Mr Marsh was staring over Marty's head.

"Happy birthday!" Theresa said to him. "I've brought you a present."

"Thank you!" Mr Marsh looked at his daughters. He didn't seem to know what to do.

Star was gazing at Clare with his bright midnight eyes, and she was gazing back at him, unable to look away. It was almost as if she were under a spell. Then she looked up at Theresa and said, "Would you like to come in and have some cake?"

"Yes, please," said Theresa Tree.

A great big smile spread itself across Mr Marsh's face. A real smile. His birthday wish had come true.

THE

END